# THE GREEN GIANT

## KATIE COTTLE

**PAVILION**

*Pavilion team:*
Neil Dunnicliffe, Harriet Grylls, Anna Lubecka

*Text and illustrations:*
© Katie Cottle 2019

First published in the UK in 2019 by Pavilion Children's Books, 43 Great Ormond Street, London, WC1N 3HZ. An imprint of Pavilion Books Company Limited. The moral rights of the author and illustrator have been asserted. All rights reserved. No part of this publication may be reproduced, stored in a retrieval system, or transmitted in any form or by any means electronic, mechanical, photocopying, recording or otherwise, without prior permission of the copyright owner. ISBN: 9781843654001. A CIP catalogue record for this book is available from the British Library. 10 9 8 7 6 5 4 3 2 1 Reproduction by Mission, Hong Kong. Printed by 1010 Printing International Ltd, China. This book can be ordered directly from the publisher online at www.pavilionbooks.com, or try your local bookshop.

MIX
Paper from
responsible sources
FSC® C016973

Bea Green and her sausage dog Iris

are leaving the city to visit the country.

They're going to see Grandad
for a short summer holiday.

Grandad loves
his garden.

He loves to sow
and to water,
to weed and
to mow.

Bea loves to do n o t h i n g.

And Iris loves to look out for things to chase... like...

...a cat!

"Iris, stop!"

Bea leaps up and chases after her naughty dog.

Where is she? Next door's garden
looks WILD, and Bea can't see Iris anywhere.

Climbing over the fence, Bea spots a small greenhouse
with the door wide open. Maybe Iris is in there?

Inside it is HUGE
and packed with plants.

There are
plants of
all **sizes**,
all *shapes* and
all shades of green!

Suddenly leaves start to rustle.

Louder. LOUDER.

"Phew!" It's just the cat. "Iris, where are you?"

Bea shivers. She feels like something is watching her. She's sure that can't be true.

But suddenly...

A giant, *gloomy* shadow looms over Bea.

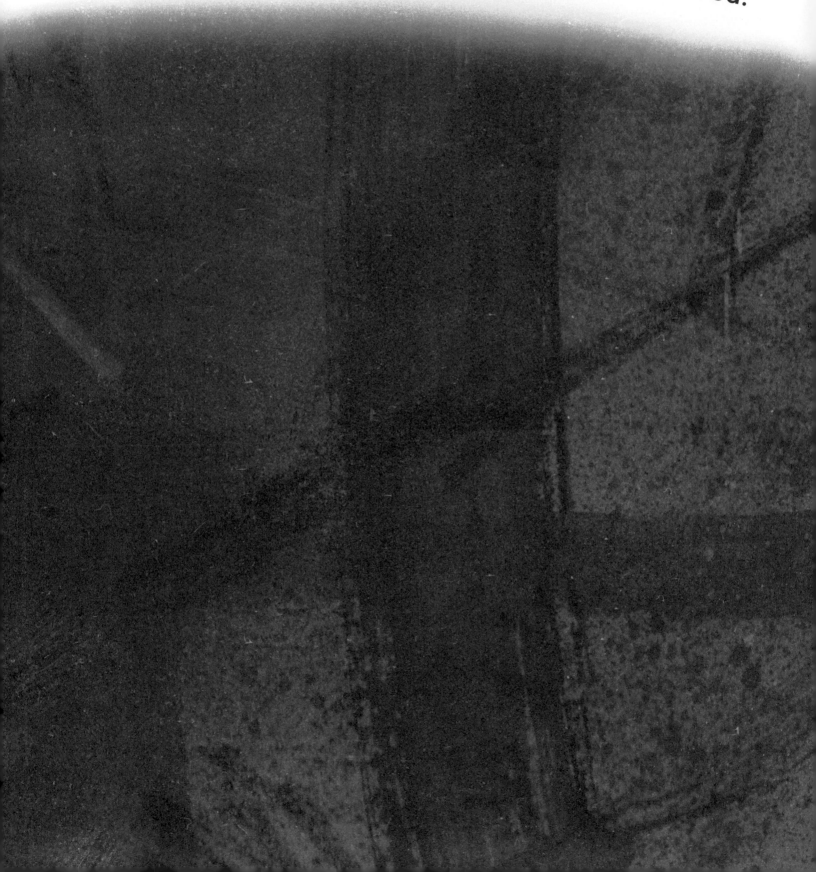

She looks up and sees...

...a giant!

A real giant!

A green giant!

It waves hello.

It seems friendly.

Gradually,
the giant tells
its story.

"I was germinated in the city and
was a happy young sapling.

"But the city got more grey and it was
hard to breathe. I had to leave."

"I eventually found this **magical** greenhouse.

We all have room
to **grow** here."

Bea had fun with her green
friends all summer long.

But too soon it
was time to leave.

"Don't be sad," said the giant.
"You know where to find me;
come back and visit."

And he gave her a present –
a handful of sparkling seeds.

Back in the city,
Bea missed the
giant and her gang
of green friends.
She noticed how
grey everything
seemed.

She looked
at her present
and sprinkled
the seeds.

With water
and sunlight,
green started
to grow...

...and grow...

...and grow.

Perhaps one day
soon the green giant
will come back to
visit the city.